ZOO CREW

Antelope Hope

BRIDGE

Written by Brenda Scott Royce

Illustrated by Joseph Wilkins

JOLLY
FiSH
PRESS

Mendota Heights, Minnesota

Book design by Sarah Taplin
Illustrations by Joseph Wilkins (Beehive Illustration)

Published in the United States by Jolly Fish Press, an imprint of North Star Editions, Inc.

First Edition
First Printing, 2022

Library of Congress Cataloging-in-Publication Data (pending)
978-1-63163-632-5 (paperback)
978-1-63163-631-8 (hardcover)

Jolly Fish Press
North Star Editions, Inc.
2297 Waters Drive
Mendota Heights, MN 55120
www.jollyfishpress.com

Printed in the United States of America

TABLE OF CONTENTS

CHAPTER 1

Meeting Bongos

"Good morning, Junior Volunteers!" Luis waved at Micah and Katy. Luis was the Mountain Bluff Zoo volunteer coordinator. The kids waved back excitedly. It was Saturday morning. They had just arrived at the zoo. The two friends were wearing their matching safari vests.

"What are we going to do today?" Katy asked.

Katy and Micah had already done a lot since they began volunteering. They'd helped prepare a habitat for new animals. They'd watched a tiger mother give birth to twin cubs. They'd also solved a mystery about the zoo's monkeys. Along the way, they had learned a great deal about animals. They'd learned about the people who take care of them, too.

"Today, you'll be working with bongos," Luis said.

"Oh, I love playing drums." Micah drummed his hands against his leg.

"Not *that* kind of bongo," Luis said with a laugh. "A bongo is also the name of an animal. It's a type of antelope."

Micah shrugged. "I've never heard of them."

"Neither have I," Katy said. "And I've seen most of the animals in this zoo." Katy's mother, Corinna, worked as an animal keeper. Katy had been visiting the zoo since she was very young.

"Well then, it's about time you meet them," Luis said. "Follow me."

"They're beautiful," Katy said when she saw the bongos. They were

reddish brown, the color of pumpkin pie. They had thin white stripes on their bodies. Their large ears pointed outward.

"Look at those big antlers," Micah said.

"Actually, they're horns," said Alisa, the bongo keeper. Alisa was a tall redhead. She reminded Katy of a flamingo. "Antlers fall off and are regrown every year. Horns grow throughout an animal's lifetime. Deer have antlers. Sheep, goats, and antelope have horns."

Micah snapped photos of the biggest bongo. "That one has huge horns."

Alisa nodded. "Almost three feet long," she said. "That's Sokoro. His mate, Makena, is over in the corner. The little one next to her is Jim."

"Sokoro and Makena sound like African names," Katy noted.

"Great observation," Alisa said. "Mountain bongos live in the forests of Kenya in East Africa. So, we gave them Kenyan names. *Sokoro* means 'lucky one.' *Makena* means 'happy one.'"

"What does *Jim* mean?" Micah asked.

"His full name is *Jimiyu.* That means 'born during summer.' We call him Jim for short." Alisa led them to a shed next to the bongo enclosure. She handed each of the kids a rake. "Now, let's get to work."

CHAPTER 2

At Risk

Katy and Micah spent the morning cleaning the enclosure. They raked up dead leaves, broken branches, and bongo poop. They filled a wheelbarrow with the waste. As they worked, Alisa taught them all about bongos.

"Bongos are great at camouflage," she said. "Those thin stripes help them blend into the forest. That helps the bongos hide from predators. Sadly,

Kenya's forests are disappearing." The keeper frowned. "So are mountain bongos. They're almost extinct in the wild."

Katy gasped. "Really?" she said. They've almost died out? How many are left?"

"Probably less than one hundred. There are actually more bongos in zoos than in the wild."

"That's sad," Micah said. "Why are they in zoos at all?"

Alisa set down her rake. "That's a great question. Zoos often take care of endangered animals. The zoos help protect them. If bongos vanish from the wild, they can still survive. Zoos have even returned some types of animals to the wild. The mountain bongo is one of those."

Alisa lifted the handles of the

wheelbarrow. "I'll take this to the compost bin. You two get washed up. Then we'll feed the bongos."

When Alisa came back, she was pushing a different wheelbarrow. This one was filled with alfalfa hay. Micah and Katy helped spread it around the yard. Then the kids gave each bongo an apple. The bongos ate the apples from the palms of their hands.

"These bongos love apples." Then Alisa pointed at the trees dotting the yard. "They also eat leaves from those

ficus trees. We try to give them the same foods they'd eat in the wild. Or as close as we can." She hung a salt lick from a tree branch. "In the wild, they visit natural salt licks. Their diet of leaves and plants doesn't contain the sodium their bodies need."

"You know a lot about how they live in the wild," Micah noted.

Alisa nodded. "In college, I traveled to Kenya to study bongos."

"Wow!" Katy's eyes widened. "How many did you see?"

"Not very many," Alisa answered.

"Bongos are very rare—and very good at hiding. It was difficult to spot them in the forest. Mostly, I found snares and removed them. That way, they couldn't hurt the animals."

"Snares?" Micah frowned. "You're not talking about snare drums, are you?"

Alisa shook her head. "This kind of snare is a trap. Hunters hide them in the forest. The snares catch and kill animals."

"I thought that their forest homes are disappearing," Katy said. "And that's why bongos are endangered."

"That's one of the main problems they face. The other is poaching. That's what we call illegal hunting."

Katy looked at the bongos. Makena and Jim were munching on hay. Sokoro stripped leaves off a tree branch with his tongue. They were so beautiful and peaceful. Katy felt sad. She thought of the other bongos being hunted in the wild.

CHAPTER 3

How to Help?

On the drive home, Micah told his father about their day. He described the bongos and their tree-filled yard. Then he shared what they'd learned about poachers.

"Before today, we'd never even heard of bongos," Katy said. "They almost disappeared before we'd even seen one!"

"It's really sad," Micah said. "Most

people don't know they exist. So, how can they protect them?"

Micah's father shrugged. "Maybe *you* can think of a way to help."

"We are helping them," Micah said. "We cleaned up all their poop!"

His father chuckled. "Yes, you two are helping the zoo's bongos. Maybe you can also help them in the wild."

"I don't see how," Micah said.

"Kenya is so far away," Katy added. "We can't just go search for snares like Alisa did. Maybe when we're older."

Micah stared out the car window.

He let out a sigh. "By that time, they might all be gone."

CHAPTER 4

A Great Idea

Sunday morning, Micah and Katy were back at the bongo enclosure. As they raked, they tried to think of ways to help.

"We can raise money," Katy said. "And send it to the people who protect the forests."

Micah nodded. "They could hire more helpers to search for snares."

The kids shared their idea with Alisa.

The keeper was filling the bongos' drinking pond with fresh water. She looked up from her task. "A fundraiser is a good idea. It should be something fun. That way lots of people will want to come."

"My dad's fire station does lots of charity events," Micah said. "Charity events raise money for good causes. My favorite one is bingo night."

Katy smiled. "I love playing bingo. I bet we could get tons of people to come. Especially if they know it will help the bongos."

"I know!" Micah bounced on the balls of his feet. "We'll call it 'Bingo for Bongos!'"

CHAPTER 5

Bongo Bingo

"G-52!" Micah's father said. His voice boomed through the zoo's event room. He'd volunteered to be the bingo caller. The room was packed with people of all ages.

Katy and Micah looked at the bingo cards in front of them. "Got it," Katy said. She placed a plastic chip on the number.

Three weeks had passed since the

kids first hatched their plan. Alisa helped them put it together. They made flyers for the Bingo for Bongos event. They used Micah's photos and Katy's drawings of the bongos. They put the flyers all over the neighborhood. That helped spread the word about the event.

Katy's mother asked local businesses to donate prizes. Other zookeepers did, too. People bought tickets to take part in the bingo. Some people also donated extra money. All the money raised would go to help bongos in the wild. The kids also created special bingo cards. Each card had facts about bongos printed on the back.

Alisa stopped by their table. "The bongo bingo cards are a big hit!"

"Thanks," Katy said. "We wanted people to learn about bongos. Even if we don't raise much money."

Mr. Draper shouted the next number, "B-11." A woman at a nearby table leaped up. "Bingo!" Everyone cheered. Katy and Micah cleared their cards for the next game.

A couple hours later, all the prizes had been won. The kids helped Alisa count the money they'd raised in ticket sales and donations. Then they handed a slip of paper to Micah's father.

"Thanks to everyone for coming," Mr. Draper said. "And for playing Bingo for Bongos. Tonight's event raised three thousand and seventy-two dollars for bongo conservation!"

Katy smiled from ear to ear. "Can you believe it, Micah?" she shouted over the applause. "A few weeks ago, we didn't even know what a bongo was!"

"I thought they were drums," Micah said. He tapped a beat on the table.

"Now we're helping to save them in the wild." Katy pointed around the crowded room. "Everyone here is helping."

Micah nodded. "I wonder what animal we can help next?"

THINK ABOUT IT

 A bongo's thin stripes help it hide in the forest. That helps it stay safe from predators. Can you think of other animals that use camouflage?

 Katy and Micah learn that the mountain bongo is endangered. They also learn that poaching and forest loss are main reasons why. Look up other endangered species. What is putting them at risk?

Katy and Micah raise money for bongos in the wild. Can you think of a way you can help animals in danger of extinction?

ABOUT THE AUTHOR

Brenda Scott Royce is the author of more than twenty books for adults and children. Animals are her favorite subject to write about. She has worked as a chimpanzee keeper at an animal sanctuary and traveled on wildlife expeditions to Africa and South America. In her free time, she helps injured birds as a volunteer with SoCal Parrot Rescue.

ABOUT THE ILLUSTRATOR

Joseph Wilkins is an illustrator living and working in the seaside town of Brighton, England. A graduate of Falmouth College of Arts in Cornwall, Joseph has spent the last fifteen years forging a successful freelance career. When not drawing, he can be found messing around with bicycles or on the beach with his family.

DOGGIE DAYCARE
IS OPEN FOR BUSINESS!

Join siblings Shawn and Kat Choi as they start their own pet-sitting service out of their San Francisco home. Every dog they meet has its own special personality, sending the kids on fun (and furry) adventures all over the city!

"Shawn and Kat are supported by a diverse cast in which readers of many colors can see themselves reflected. Problem-solvers and dog lovers alike will pounce on this series." —*Kirkus Reviews*

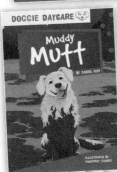